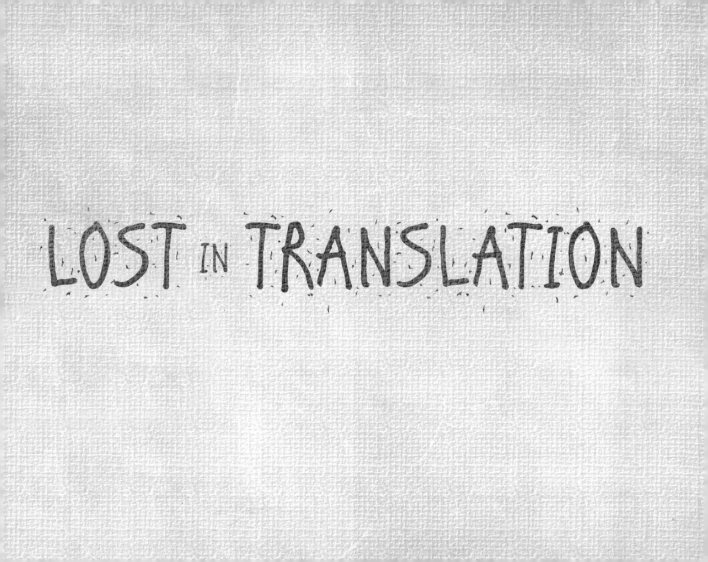

First published in the United Kingdom in 2012 by
Portico Books
10 Southcombe Street
London
W14 0RA

An imprint of Anova Books Company Ltd

ISBN 9781907554551

A CIP catalogue record for this book is available from the British Library.

10 9 8 7 6 5 4 3 2 1

Reproduction by Mission Productions, Hong Kong
Printed and bound by Toppan Leefung Printing, China

This book can be ordered direct from the publisher at
www.anovabooks.com

CHRIS STONE

LOST IN TRANSLATION

THE ENGLISH LANGUAGE TAKEN HOSTAGE AT HOME AND ABROAD

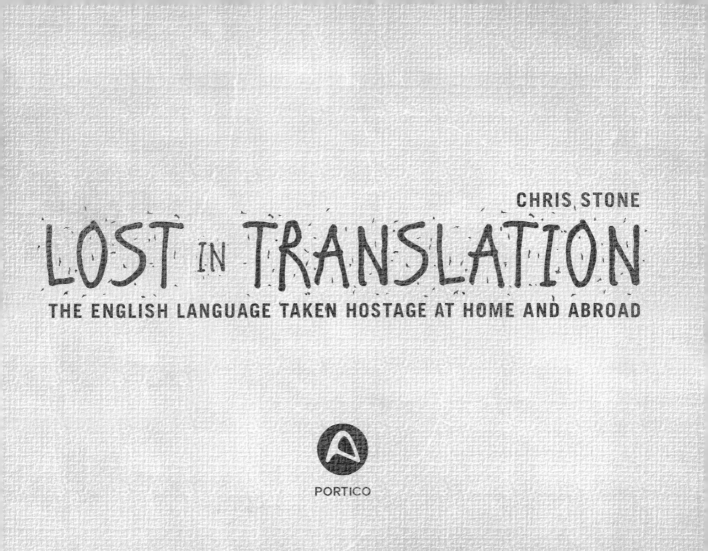

PORTICO

WELCOME TO LOST IN TRANSLATION ...

Members are requested to leave their shoes with ego outside the office.

No matter where you go in the world, the English language is constantly held hostage at the hands of the billions of global speakers who abuse it, beat it up and toss it aside as if just another tragic victim of a modern crime. The English language is broken. And while that's a crying shame, as it turns out, it's also bloody hilarious.

The book you are holding in your hands has not been designed to insult people whose native language is not English. If anything this book makes more fun of the people whose native language *is* English and mangle it just as badly. So please don't take offence. This book's intention is to make fun of *everyone* regardless of whether you live in Japan, Jordan or Jermany. It is an international insight into the world's most-travelled language, the mess it is in and the lengths (intentional or not) some people have gone to mistreat it. From terrible tourist sign translations to sloppy menu spellchecking to just plain incompetence, *Lost in Translation* demonstrates how one of the most prestigious languages on the planet is treated when it goes on holiday. But it's not just abroad that these criminal activities occur.

They happen on home turf too, right under our very noses and they are no less a serious threat to the future of the language. Everywhere you look these days there is bad language, worse English and a veritable buffet of ridiculousness and mis-understanding that will make you laugh ... and then cry. Indeed, if Britain is becoming as illiterate as all the British newspapers constantly make out that it is, then this book should, hopefully, make people realise that the whole world is going to the dogs and there is simply nothing you can do about it except laugh.

So, join us on this trip around the world where a cacophony of international calamities, as well as an assortment of home-grown, horrific wordplay, should help remind you that the English language is forever at the mercy of those who speak it. It is a language constantly lost in translation ... never to be found again.

Friday's M e n u

"Fish Bar £2.45 "
You Have The Choice Of Cod Or Baterd
Haddcock Or For The Halther Eater You Can
Have Your Fish Just Plan Griled

Chips £0.90
Mushy Peas £0.40

TRADING ASUSAL

'Never make fun of someone who speaks broken English. It means they know another language.'

H. Jackson Brown, Jr.

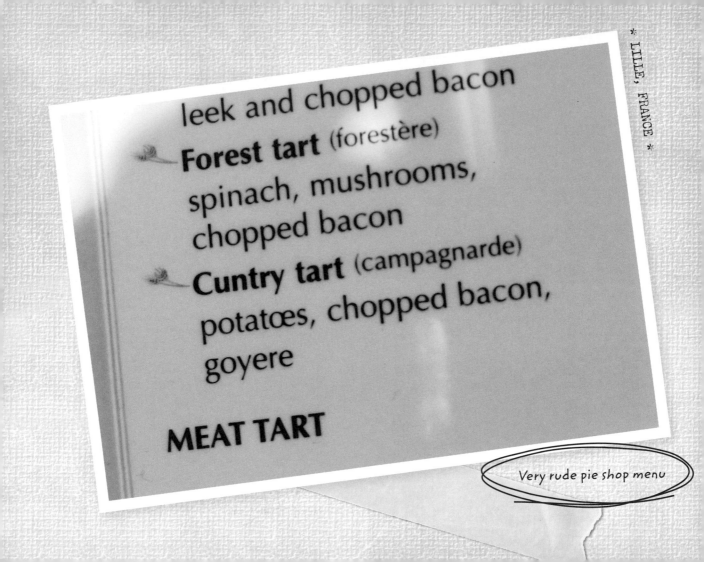

leek and chopped bacon

Forest tart (forestère)
spinach, mushrooms, chopped bacon

Cuntry tart (campagnarde)
potatœs, chopped bacon, goyere

MEAT TART

Very rude pie shop menu

Carful! Falling thing

* CHINA *

Which way again?, Orta (possibly)

ห้ามผ่าน
ใช้สำหรับขนสินค้าผ่านและคนพิการเท่านั้น
No ENTRY
ONLY Product Carry
and Handicaps are allowed

MBK
CENTER

* INDIA *

Politically incorrect
terminology!

FUTURE VETERANS OF AMREICA

Star spangld bannr, Minnesota

USA

It looks like they've sold out of K's and A's too, Oxford Street, London, UK

Keep what?, London, UK

JORDAN

غرفة العباءات
للعرب والأجانب
PUTTING-ON SPECIAL
CLOTHES ROOM

Good news for Clark Kent, confusing for the rest of us!

Balesetveszély miatt
a romkert falain sétálni
szigorúan tilos!

Along of dangerous accident
to walk on the walls
in the garden of ruin
is strictly forbidden!

HUNGARY

Yoda sign-writing skills
they have, Hungary

Straight to the point, Dubai

ATM LOL!

SPAIN

GALICIA

AMOUNT WITHDRAWN

The amount keyed in is

200,00EUR

If correct: press **ANNOTATION**
If incorrect: press **CORRECT**

Paying less is a gift at Christmas

THESE BRUSHES ARE NOT TESTERS PLEASE ASK STAFF FOR ASSISTANTS

Further help required, Sydney, Australia

Take the bus, Waterloo station, London

No apology necessary

CHINA

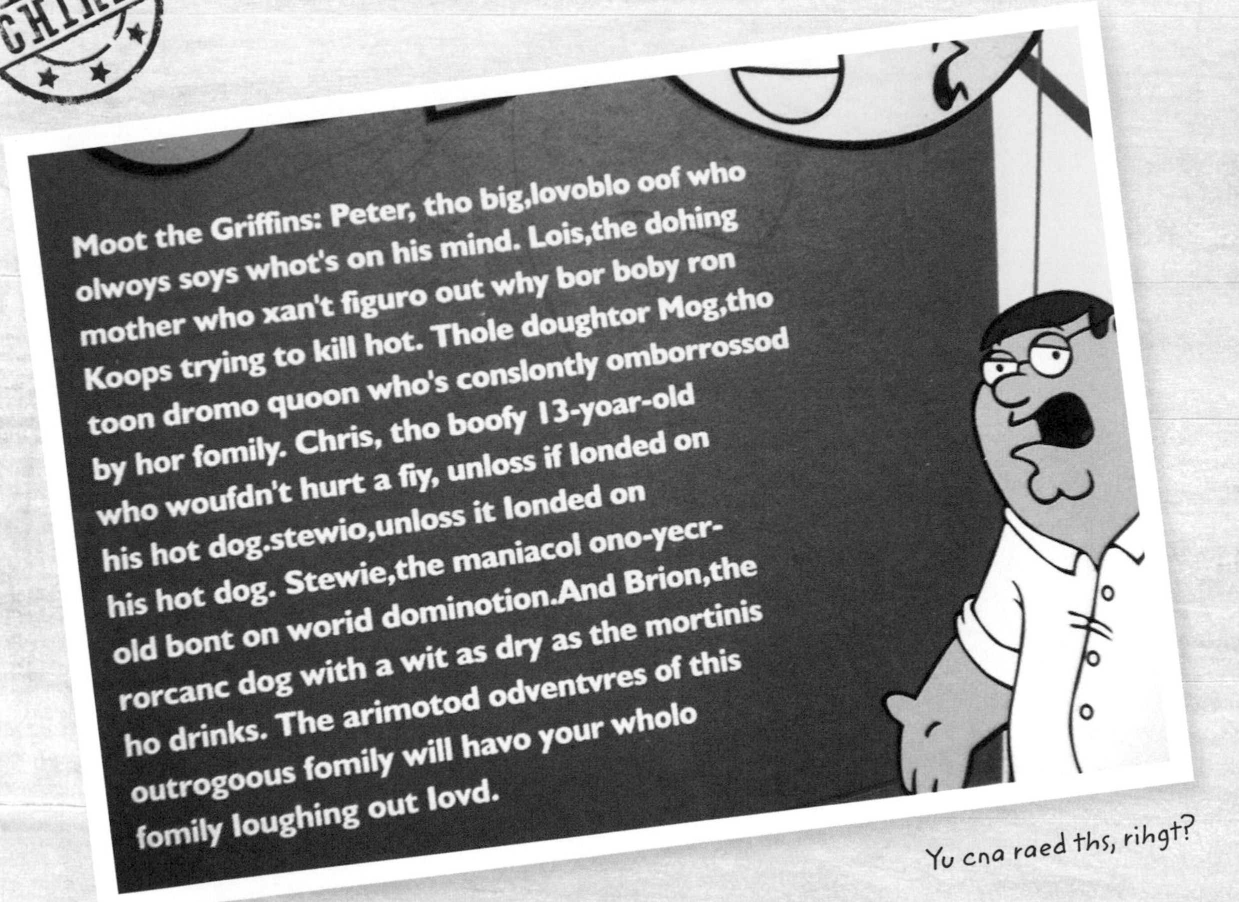
Moot the Griffins: Peter, tho big,lovoblo oof who
olwoys soys whot's on his mind. Lois,the dohing
mother who xan't figuro out why bor boby ron
Koops trying to kill hot. Thole doughtor Mog,tho
toon dromo quoon who's conslontly omborrossod
by hor fomily. Chris, tho boofy 13-yoar-old
who woufdn't hurt a fiy, unloss if londed on
his hot dog.stewio,unloss it londed on
his hot dog. Stewie,the maniacol ono-yecr-
old bont on worid dominotion.And Brion,the
rorcanc dog with a wit as dry as the mortinis
ho drinks. The arimotod odventvres of this
outrogoous fomily will havo your wholo
fomily loughing out lovd.

Yu cna raed ths, rihgt?

(Spring roll)

มันฝรั่งทอด

(French fried)

ไข่เจียว/ปู/กุ้ง/หมูสับ

(Omelet with crap/prawn/pork)

เอ็นข้อไก่ทอด

KEEP CLEAR OF THE
CRAP OMELETTE!

* KO LANTA *

THAILAND

GENUINE FAKE WATCHES

* TURKEY *

Genuine or fake honesty?

Well, that's one way to say goodbye, Thailand

旅 客 下 车
Passenger   Got off

Network Rail Engineering Work
Affecting CrossCountry Services
Sunday 25th April 2010
Cambridge - Stansted Airport

CrossCountry Services will operate
between Birmingham New Street and
Cambridge. Replacement toad
transport will operate between
Cambridge and Stansted Airport.

Replacement toad transport,
Carlisle station, Wales

Incorrect use of a pronoun, Simla, India

Fish Burger.....................................

Mixed Burger (viande , poulet) ...

Œuf Burger (œuf, viande)...........

Cheez Oeuf Burger (viande, oeuf,

Ass Hamburger (viande, salade, ch

Ass Cheez Burger (viande, froma

salade, frite)..........................

SALAD

Mixed salades ....

I think I'll have the salad, Senegal

愛我，別惹我

Love me ,don't bother me.

私を愛してくれて、
怒らせないでください。

CHINA

Or in other words – DON'T TOUCH!

请不要攀扶
Don't speel

CHINA

What the hell is Speeling?
Because the picture doesn't give any clues!

Anyone for takeaway?

* BUDAPEST *

"PELIGRO ¡NO PASAR!"
"DANGER NE PAS ARRIVER!"
"I AM IN DANGER, NOT TO HAPPEN!"
"ICH BIN IN GEFAHR, NICHT ZU GESCHEHEN!

"Prohibido el paso a toda persona ajena a la obra"
"Interpit le pas à chaque persnne étrangére au travail"
"Prohibited the step to every person foreing to the work"

In summary: please do not climb over their fence, Granada

* SPAIN *

USA

Vowel movement!

ROCKET

ELECTRICAL

* CALIFORNIA *

Lame Mirror

ラメミラー／M

Size 約11.6×10cm

CARTOON Expression

CHINA

Non-reflecting mirror?

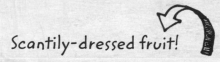

Stuffed paprika with rice 1890.-
and minced pork

Chicken stew mixed with 2990.-
rice in spring

Veal stew in Paprika style 2990.-
with noodles

Apple in dressing gown 890.-

HUNGARY

เมีที่ว่างสำหรับคนไทยเสมอ

Don't Serve Dog,Cat,Rat,Wrm

An instruction or what's missing from the menu?

wHAT IS A WRM?

A good nigth out guaranteed!, Chile

ATTENZIONE ALZARE I PIEDI
ATTENTION LEVER LES PIEDS

PLEASE TAKE OFF THE FEET
VORSICHTIG DIE FÜSSE ERHEBEN

VIETATO SCENDERE

ITALY

Painful sacrifice just to go skiing!

This Balham café puts a new spin on noodles, London

UK

Aubergine with pork mince would surely be much tastier?

温馨提示
Warm prompt
请关好
车辆门窗
Watch your valuables.

N4 Aborigine with pork mince

Tourists — You have been warmed!

Slippery over-fives are a nightmare in France!

ATTENTION GLISSANT
INTERDIT AUX + 5 ANS

BEWARE SLIPPERY
PEOPLE OVER FIVE
NOT ALLOWED

TXALUPA

* FRANCE *

☆ Insensitive advertising, USA ☆

Vacancy Waitress

- Panctual
- Friendly
- Good english
- Smart

Give your CV or leave your detail inside

LONDON, UK

Irony alert! Irony alert! Irony alert! Irony alert!

PERU

TASTES GREAT WITH CHIPS!

That's a bum deal!

Poetic justice!

* KENT, UK *

...brings results **Local news for**
KM **local people**

Pervert
trapped
by
poem

Prestige card

Any in shopping empress in three days, such as meet Take-up a post what quality problem can with this card till cent Sell place to replace.

1. The customer has to return to an original shopping store to c arry on Replace;
2. Each goods can only change goods once;
3. Change goodsthe goods which be limited by same goods number;
4. Already dress, or is damage, or through fix
   Goods of change forgive not to replace.

The my plant reserve to aut-henticate, goods whether There is the right that the above circ-umstance appear.

The harbor Jun system dress product of honor

PRODUCT AWARENESS. SAY WHAT?!

!!!

Breakfast
Lunch
Tossed Salad

Sandwiches
Wraps
Smooties

Not-so-smooth signwriting skills

Romantic advice... from a sign

IMPORTANTE

TENERSI
SALDAMENTE
ALLE MANIGLIE
DI SICUREZZA

TO FIRMLY
HOLD HIM TO
THE SAFETY
HANDLES

* ITALY *

CLAIM RIGHT

We kindly ask our honoured clients for finding of shortages and open defects to check the devices in the check-out area after their payment.
Claims for open defects and shortages after leaving the store would be incorrect.

Claims for thinking this sign made sense would be incorrect!

Ah, the perils of using Google Translate, Bolivia

lo fruta todos los que estén con el intestino y estómago delicado.
BUENOS HIJOS DEL SEÑOR · DIOS LOS BENDIGA A TODOS.

"EL HUERTO" RECOMMENDS TO BE CAREFUL TO HIS RESPECTABLE CLIENTELE, BEING YOU BELONGED BECAUSE IT OF WANTING BECOMES RESPONSIBLE FOR NONE OBJECT LOST OR STOLE RESTAURANT INSIDE.

THE MANAGEMENT

ประชาสัมพันธ์

สำนักพระราชวัง
เปิดให้บริการผู้เข้าชมพระบรมมหาราชวัง
ทุกวัน ตั้งแต่เวลา ๐๘.๓๐ น. ถึง ๑๕.๓๐ น.
สำนักพระราชวัง สงวนสิทธิ์ในการเปิด-ปิด
โดยไม่ต้องแจ้งให้ทราบล่วงหน้า

THE GRAND PALACE & THE EMERALD BUDDHA TEMPLE
IS OPEN EVERYDAY FROM 8.30 a.m. UNTIL 3.30 p.m.

DO NOT TRUST WILY STRANGERS

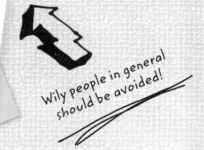

Wily people in general
should be avoided!

THAILAND

'Keep Clear' would be better advice

* MASADA, ISRAEL *

אין מעבר
שטח עתיקות

NO THOROUGHFARE
ANTIQUITIES

Seriously, don't drink the water!

SINGAPORE *

出口 EXIT 출구

またのお越しをお待ちしております。
We will wait for the next coming.

喫煙所
Smoking Area

JAPAN

That's nice, but you might have a long wait!

ALL OUR BOXED EASTER EGGS
PACKAGING IS REUSABLE,
RECYCLABLE OR HOME COMPOSTABLE

CLOSING

HUGH
SAVING
50%

Who is Hugh Saving?

* LONDON, UK *

GEEN TOEGANG
NO ENTRY
TRESPASSERS
WILL BECOME
PROSTITUTES

SOUTH AFRICA

Let's hope they mean
'prosecuted'!

No
ishing

Beware
Srong
currents

No
swimn

Taxpayers' money floating out to sea!

UK

GELLÉRT ↗
BAD-SWIMMING POOL-SPA

The far more popular 'Good' swimming pool is on the left!

BUSINSSN
FOR SALE
SELLING OUT
EVERY THING
GOING OUT
BUSINSSN
2 WHEELES
SHOPE CART
10 00 8 00
4 WHEELES
18 00 12 00

LET'S HOPE THEIR SPELLING HAD NOTHING TO DO WITH WHY THEY ARE 'GOING OUT BUSINSSN'!

* NEW YORK *

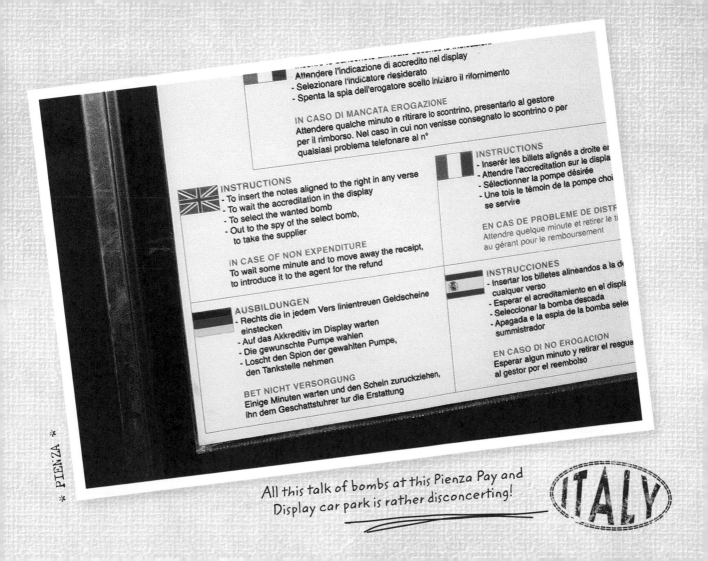

- Attendere l'indicazione di accredito nel display
- Selezionare l'indicatore desiderato
- Spenta la spia dell'erogatore scelto iniziare il rifornimento

IN CASO DI MANCATA EROGAZIONE
Attendere qualche minuto e ritirare lo scontrino, presentarlo al gestore per il rimborso. Nel caso in cui non venisse consegnato lo scontrino o per qualsiasi problema telefonare al n°

INSTRUCTIONS
- To insert the notes aligned to the right in any verse
- To wait the accreditation in the display
- To select the wanted bomb
- Out to the spy of the select bomb, to take the supplier

IN CASE OF NON EXPENDITURE
To wait some minute and to move away the recaipt, to introduce it to the agent for the refund

AUSBILDUNGEN
- Rechts die in jedem Vers linientreuen Geldscheine einstecken
- Auf das Akkreditiv im Display warten
- Die gewunschte Pumpe wahlen
- Loscht den Spion der gewahlten Pumpe, den Tankstelle nehmen

BET NICHT VERSORGUNG
Einige Minuten warten und den Schein zuruckziehen, ihn dem Geschattstuhrer tur die Erstattung

INSTRUCTIONS
- Inserér les billets alignés a droite er
- Attendre l'accreditation sur le displa
- Sélectionner la pompe désirée
- Une tois le témoin de la pompe choi se servire

EN CAS DE PROBLEME DE DISTR
Attendre quelque minute et retirer le ti au gérant pour le remboursement

INSTRUCCIONES
- Insertar los billetes alineandos a la de cualquier verso
- Esperar el acreditamiento en el displa
- Seleccionar la bomba descada
- Apagada e la espia de la bomba sele summistrador

EN CASO DI NO EROGACION
Esperar algun minuto y retirar el resgua al gestor por el reembolso

PIENZA

All this talk of bombs at this Pienza Pay and Display car park is rather disconcerting!

ITALY

BABY URINATE

Short and to the point.
And if baby won't go,
make it!

CHINA

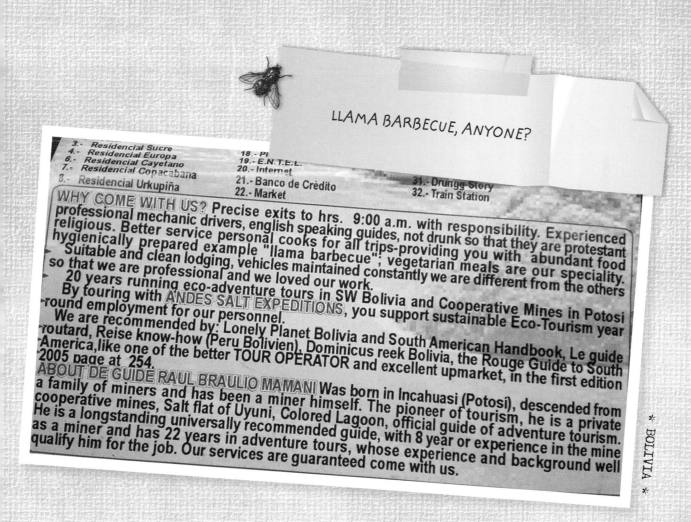

LLAMA BARBECUE, ANYONE?

3.- Residencial Sucre
4.- Residencial Europa
6.- Residencial Cayetano
7.- Residencial Copacabana
8.- Residencial Urkupiña

18.- P...
19.- E.N.T.E.L.
20.- Internet
21.- Banco de Crédito
22.- Market

31.- Drungg Story
32.- Train Station

WHY COME WITH US? Precise exits to hrs. 9:00 a.m. with responsibility. Experienced professional mechanic drivers, english speaking guides, not drunk so that they are protestant religious. Better service personal cooks for all trips-providing you with abundant food hygienically prepared example "llama barbecue"; vegetarian meals are our speciality. Suitable and clean lodging, vehicles maintained constantly so that we are different from the others so that we are professional and we loved our work.

20 years running eco-adventure tours in SW Bolivia and Cooperative Mines in Potosi By touring with **ANDES SALT EXPEDITIONS**, you support sustainable Eco-Tourism year-round employment for our personnel.

We are recommended by: Lonely Planet Bolivia and South American Handbook, Le guide routard, Reise know-how (Peru Bolivien), Dominicus reek Bolivia, the Rouge Guide to South America, like one of the better TOUR OPERATOR and excellent upmarket, in the first edition 2005 page at 254.

ABOUT DE GUIDE RAUL BRAULIO MAMANI Was born in Incahuasi (Potosi), descended from a family of miners and has been a miner himself. The pioneer of tourism, he is a private cooperative mines, Salt flat of Uyuni, Colored Lagoon, official guide of adventure tourism. He is a longstanding universally recommended guide, with 8 year or experience in the mine as a miner and has 22 years in adventure tours, whose experience and background well qualify him for the job. Our services are guaranteed come with us.

* BOLIVIA *

American's may pronounce GARAGE differently,
but it's spelt the same — better than 'ger raj' though!

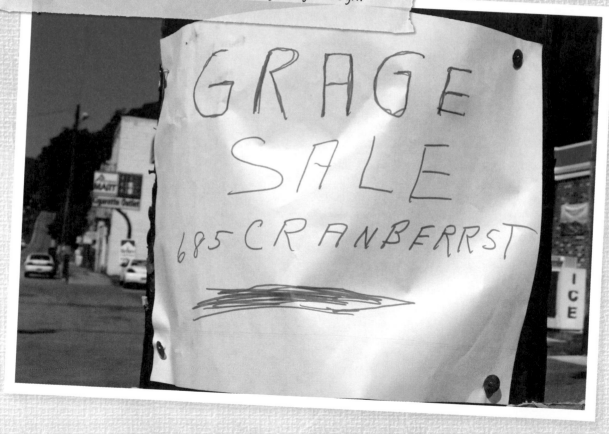

A VASÚT VESZÉLYES ÜZEM! KÉRJÜK TESTI ÉPSÉGÜKRE FOKOZOTTAN ÜGYELJENEK!

DIE BAHN IST EIN GEFÄHRLICHER BETRIEB! ACH VTEN SIE BITTE AUF IHREN KÖRPERLICHEN GESUNDHEIT!

THE RAILWAY IS A DANGEROUS MILL! PLEASE PAY ATTENTION TO YOUR BODILY FEAR!

HUNGARY

ALWAYS PAY ATTENTION TO YOUR BODILY FEAR!

* SINGAPORE *

A hotel where you pay more...
for a cheaper price?

おことわり
Notice

本日二の丸庭園の滝が、工事に伴い水を
流しておりません。
何卒ご了承ください。

TODAY IS UNDER CONSTRUCTION
THANK YOU FOR UNDERSTANDING.

JAPAN

Better go to bed and wait for tomorrow then!

万 花 楼
CHAMBER OF TEN THOUSAND FLOWERS
卫 生 间
TOILET →

Surely they could have made two signs?

This treat always goes down well, China

This SIGN shop has clearly got the wrong end of the stick!

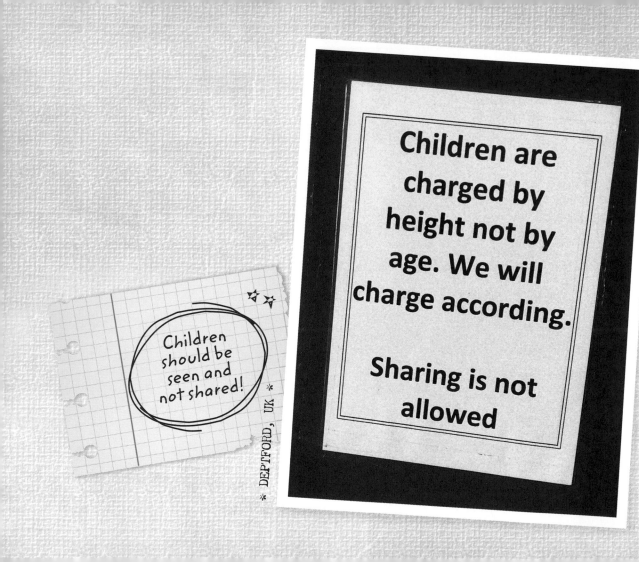

Fruit that makes you feel good

SWEET CHEERY £ 1.99

No! Anything but the treacherous acts ... on an escalator!

CHINA

WATCH YOUR STEP

请勿逆行

PLEASE NOT THE TREACHEROUS ACTS

干锅茶树菌菇土鸡　48元/例

28元/例

干鍋、平鍋

Hotpot Less soup, more fat, rich flavor.

一场辣的享受

38元/例

Appreciate the honesty, but we'd rather have more of the soup and less of the fat!

只有行为美，
花草才更美！

Good behavior makes grasses
and flowers more beautiful!

That seems rather an ambitious claim, but if they say so ..., China

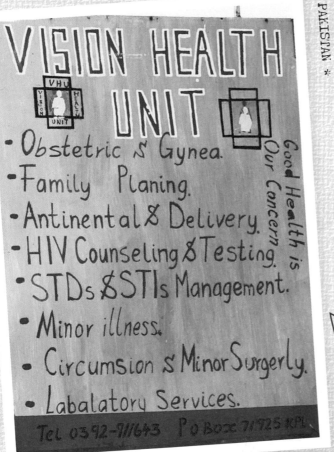

監巴繹度地中海美食餐廳

炙烤南級冰魚佐酸荳塔塔醬 **430**
South roasts the level whitebait to assist the tower sauce

阿爾薩斯蒜蒸香榭鱈魚 **450**
The Alsace garlic steams the fragrant pavilion cod

碳烤墨西哥風味迷迭春雞 **450**
The carbon roasts the Mexican flavor to confuse the bamboo chicken to assist the gentle breeze sauce

炙烤 P.S 沙朗牛排襯洋芋塔 **50**
Roasts the P.S grain sand bright beefsteak lining potato tower.

經典酥烤俄利崗酸菜德國豬腳 **5**
The Classics crisply roast the German knuckle to attachthe Russia advantage hillock pickled cabbage

板煎美國 Prime 無骨牛小排.....

COULD I HAVE THE GERMAN KNUCKLE PLEASE ...
BUT HOLD THE HILLOCK PICKLED CABBAGE?

* TAIWAN *

消火栓
FIRE HOSE RANT

WATCH OUT! IT MIGHT EXPLODE!

IRAN

Khosro Abad Building
In 12.23 A.H The great Aman_allah_Khan the gove
rnor of kurdestan during The Qajar Dynasty Rei
gn ordered the construction of this buiding This co
mplex has two sections The main parts with colum
ned entrance In the west wing and eastern sectio
n with columned balconies over the yard of the
building and it has outer space too. other sections
are bathrooms gate men and servants room
Decoration of the buildin include moulding plaster
beautiful A rosi and a cross shaped pool made of sto
ne in the yard

Registration No 1491

SAY IT FIVE TIMES FAST!

This Iranian sign officially contains the world's longest word!

The Bible should be renamed the Bibly!

CHAPEL OF PEACE
THE BEST KNOWN CHAPEL IN THE NECROPOLIS
FROM THE 5TH OR 6TH CENTIERY A·D
MANY SUBJEITS FROM THE BIBLY
ARE PAINTED ON ITS DOME SUCH AS
ADOM AND EVE, ABRAHAM AND HIS SON
SYMBOLS OF PEACE & JUSTICE ST. PAUL & TEKLA &
ARK OF NOAH ....

* EGYPT *

CAFE
BONEFIDE GRILLS
IF YOU WANT TO
YOU MAY COOK YOURSELF

Thanks for the offer, but we'd prefer a burger!

OH DEAR!, Loughborough, UK

CAUTION
NATURAL
TRAIL
U EVEN
SURFACE

The importance of the letter N, Washington State

Sadly, the pictures don't make it any more appetising!

享受一份独特　ENJOY EACH UNIQUE

Cold juice with no features such as non-greasy, fragrance about muscle penetration, the more people eat more incense chewing.

冷菜具有无汁无腻等特点，讲究香料透入肌里，使人食之越嚼越香。

* CHINA *

Михайловский сад
закрыт на просушку

The Mikhailovsky garden
is closed for drying

Hair dryers
at the ready!

THAILAND

Bangkok taxi sign — clearly no farting allowed!

'I'll have a number 6... what is it?'

데기야끼 정식

GRILL ELL CHICKEN WITH RICE

5 煎鸡肉套餐
鳥の唐揚げ定食
후라이드치킨 정식   **18** 元

FRIED CHICKEN

6 炸鸡肉套餐
チキンカツチーズ定食
치킨까스치즈롤 정식   **20** 元

GREAM CHEESE CHICKEN ROW

7 奶酪鸡排套餐
エビフテイ定食
새우 튀김 정식   **20** 元

FRIED PRAWN SET

炸大虾套餐

ライスセット **PLATTER** 拼盘

8 鳥唐揚げ白身魚フライ
후라이드치킨과 돼지고기셋트   **20** 元

**FRIEC CHICKEN MEAT IS WITH THE
FISHN CHIPS PLATTER**

炸鸡肉和炸鱼排拼盘

9 トンカツ+イカ唐揚げ
튀긴돼지고기티오징어셋트   **20** 元

**FRY THE PORK STEAK WITH FRY
PARTICULARLY FISH PLATTER**

炸猪排和炸鱿鱼拼盘

10 チーブヒしカツ+コロッケ
치즈돼지고기와 치즈닭고기   **20** 元

**CREAM CHEESE PORK STEAK IS WITH
THE SOIL BEAN CAKE PLATTER**

奶酪猪排和土豆饼拼盘

CHINA

£1 each

Six for Six Pound

BARGAIN!
No wait, hang on...

* SOUTH AFRICA *

DIFFERENTLY ABLED PARKING

Ridiculous political correctness!

ID REQUIRED
DONT WASTE OUR TIME

-No young children
aloud on the premises

-Cash payment to made
prior to being tattoed!

The perfect gift
for Christmass

Get a Tattoo and peircing
voucher for the altimate
gift this year !!!!

This sign is the
'altimate' gift that
keeps on giving this
'Christmass'...

موقف سيارات

Par King

Does this Syrian road sign direct you towards a place to park your car or the house of the local golf guru? The jury's still out...

'Tecknical' problems are the least of their worries!

CLOSE TECKNICAL PROBLEM

Dubious name for a Dubai Gas Man!

Getting it wrong every 'tine'!

乐客简餐
amuseful/happy customer easy meal

经营： 特色简餐　闽台风味　港式夜宵
特色早点　潮州卤味　金陵小吃

营业时间：全天候24小时营业

customer easy

Customer easy!

Not quite
a Happy Meal!

* CHINA *

禘禱易碎，
打碎自賠！
Destroys Oneself
Compensates

'And the prize for the most esoteric supermarket aisle sign goes to...'

This is the PVC Mobile phone Case of easy schleping and more function, This case is made with import and defended radialization material.And the qppearance is so beautiful.
The main characteristic is easy schleping, it can be hunged up at the waist, hunged up at the cervix and free holding.

Hang up at the waist: This case has steel button and high strength PC clip.
The mobile phone can be hunged up at the waist with the case. And it can be went round and round for 365

Hang up at the cervix: This case has high stretch and defended snap soft fibre sling. This sling will defend hurt to the cervix and defeng breaking.

Free holding: If you will put the mobile phone into your placket or hold in your hand, you can twise off the button of the case. Because it is so easy.

'Easy schleping'!

'Twise off the button'!

NO HATS
NO HOODIES
NO ENTRY

ADT Fire and Security

VIDEO IS RECORDED
FOR CRIME PREVENTION AND

Are they sure this is what they mean?, London, UK

WELCOME TO
HOTEL MONALISA
& RESTAURANT
TAL, MANANG

Our Services: REMEMBER US FOR FRESH FOODING &
LODGING, CLEAN TOILET, ATTACH BATHROOM, COLD & HOT WATER

* SINGAPORE *

This hostelry isn't exactly five star but when you need 'fresh fooding' there's nothing better!

JAPAN

Great alliteration, shite spelling!

おみやげの店
SHIRAKABA SHIGHT-SEEING SOUVENIR SHOP
白樺 しらかば 白樺
狸小路5丁目店

I've just had one thanks!

* BANGKOK *

Say what you see!

PHOTOGRAPHY CREDITS
From start to finish, in order of appearance.

4, 15, 76, Chris Guillebeau
  (http://chrisguillebeau.com)
5, Andy Davison
6, Richard Jones
7, 88 Steven Brandist
8, Hubert Scrase
9, 10, 75, 90 Arata Usui
  (twitter.com/rattus_rattus)
11, Caspar Smekens
12, 14 Cate Halpin
13, 20, Tim Verthein
14, Scott Fannen
16, 89, Ellen Fuoto
17, 100, Sean Allison
18, Trisha Weir
19, Roving i flickr.com
20, 112 Ed Lomas
21, Robert J Fisch
22, 93, 102, Nathan Parker
23, 46, 47, 92, 110, Claire Marshall
24, 31, 59, Jude Antony
  (Unofficialghost)
25, Lee Wise
25, 37, 52, Eunjoo Paek
26, Shashank Tripathi
  (http://shanx.com)
27, Joe Carr

28, 41, 45, 69, 79, 97, Roger Croft
29, 35, 56, 62, 70, 80, 87, 109
  MF Cappiello
30, Patrick Smith
32, Christopher Scott
33, 86, David M. Meurer
34, 64, Gregory S. Springer
36, 65, Jo Peattie
38, Kat Hasler
39, Kevin Denham
40, 73 Matthew Cross
41, Leah Milner
42, 101, Joseph Hsu
43, Nichole Davis
44, Michael Cosgrave
45, Craig Purkis
47, Ross Blake
48, Leo Roubos
49, Diana Trent
50, Sarah Norman
51, Diana Naaman
51, aG Silvergirl
53, Samuel F. Kordower Chaimson
54, 66, 107, Lee Crutchley
55, 67, 108, Kevin Moore
56, Jennifer Whitehead
57, Martina Hafner

58, Natalie Suthons
60, Kristine Paulus
61, John W. Schulze
63, Nadim Ab
68, Alex Charles
71, Sarah Biggart
72, Patrick Galvin
73, Ellyn Holloway
74, 78, Dan Rosenberg
76, Dr Jackie Thomas
77, Ian G. Jacobs
80, Michael Rank
82, William James Tychonievich
84, Peggy Reimchen
85, Suzanna Marsh
87, Lea Roberts
91, Laura Sunderland
94, Paul Howard
95, Tom Kelly
96, Toby Corkindale (Wintmute)
98, Joe Carnegie
99, Richard Pigg
103, Connie Tsang
104, Pete Birkinshaw/Binaryape
105, Patrick Dalton
106, Wessel Van Der Muelen

ACKNOWLEDGEMENTS

The publishers would like to thank the many people in the flickr community, as well as the other contributing photographers from all over the world, who were kind enough to make their photographs available for publication.

Alex Charles, Craig Purkis, Roger Croft, Dr Jackie Thomas, Ed Lomas, Leah Milner, Patrick Dalton, Paul Howard, Pete Birkinshaw, Steven Brandist, Wessel van der Muelen, Ellyn Holloway, Joseph Hsu, Jude Anthony, Leo Roubos, David M Meurer, Malcolm Bull, Caspar Smekens, John Schulz, Sarah Norman, Kevin Denham, Janna Schulze, Diana Naaman, Ellen Fuoto, Jo Peattie, Patrick Smith, Garo Kalaydjian, Mikhail Goldovskiy, David TS Fraser, Diana Trent, Erik Wilson, Gregory S Springer, gregster61, Kristine Paulus, Nichole Davis, Robert Fairchild, Sarah Biggart,

Tim Verthein, Nadim Ab, aG Silvergirl, Anya Barrett, Joe Carr, Martine Hafner, tomkellyphoto, Ian G Jacobs, Chris Guillebeau, Christopher Scott, Shashank Tripathi, Joe Carnegie, Peggy Reimchen, Sam Chaimson, Sean Allison, Suzanna Marsh, Lee Crutchley, Carla H, Eunjoo Paek, William James Tychonievich, roving i flickr, Toby Corkindale, Arata Usui, Connie Tsang, Dan Rosenberg, Nathan Parker, Kevin Moore, MF Cappiello, Scott Fannen, Jennifer Whitehead and Ross Blake.

CHEERS!